My
Best Fri...

the
SUFFRAGETTE

VOTES

FOR

WOMEN

Sally
Morgan

Illustrated by
Gareth
Conway

To my darling rebel girls, Lily and Daisy.

With special thanks to Steve Riedlinger for his kind help and
eye-opening research.

Scholastic Children's Books,
Euston House, 24 Eversholt Street,
London NW1 1DB, UK

A division of Scholastic Ltd
London ~ New York ~ Toronto ~ Sydney ~ Auckland
Mexico City ~ New Delhi ~ Hong Kong

Published in the UK by Scholastic Ltd, 2018

Text © Sally Morgan, 2018
Illustrations © Gareth Conway, 2018

ISBN 978 1407 18462 3

Printed and bound in the UK by CPI Group (UK) Ltd, Croydon, CR0 4YY

2 4 6 8 10 9 7 5 3 1

Papers used by Scholastic Children's Books are made from wood grown in
sustainable forests.

www.scholastic.co.uk

Dear Reader,

WARNING! You have in your hands some **very secret** letters. Some **super important, TOP-SECRET, do-NOT-show-them-to-ANYONE-or-certain-people-could-end-up-in-SUPER-SERIOUS-trouble** kind of letters.

When Mary and I met for the very first time in 1913, I didn't know much about the **SUFFRAGETTES** or the fight for the vote. I heard lots of people talking about it, (my Father, mostly) but I didn't really know why it was so important or why any of it should matter to me.

But Mary changed **EVERYTHING**. We became **BEST FRIENDS** and wrote letters back and forth through one of the most **IMPORTANT** years in **HISTORY. OBVIOUSLY**, we didn't know that at the time ... but we did know we were having quite the adventure and got ourselves into all kinds of trouble.

I hope you enjoy reading our letters!

Love,
Christine

Mr
Forrest

Mary
Forrest

Sarah
Forrest

Edward
Forrest

Mrs
Forrest

Mr
Sedgwick

Charles
Sedgwick

Jane Linton

Christine
Sedgwick

Mrs
Sedgwick

M. Forrest
26 Landow Road
Notting Hill
London

3rd January 1913

Dear Christine,

I hope I scribbled down your address correctly! My governess,[1] Miss Inchpole, thinks it's a wonder I can read my own writing, as she can make neither head nor tail of it. I'm starting to see what she means. Haha! It was **BEYOND WONDERFUL** to meet you outside the WSPU headquarters yesterday. I have always longed for a **REAL**, **LIVE** actual pen friend. I pretended my diary was a pen friend for a while, but it never wrote back. How <u>RUDE!</u> I hope you write back! Keeping a diary is totally different from being able to write to someone who knows exactly what it is like to be eleven years old. It's **SUCH** a frustrating age, don't you think? Old enough to understand what is going on, but too young to do anything about it. That's how I feel anyway.

Did you get in a lot of trouble with your sister? Jane, was it? She looked quite angry when she found me and my

1 A governess was employed by a family to live in the home and teach the children.

sister thawing you out beside the fire. Did you make it home for dinner?

I really don't think she had any right to be so cross. Leaving you outside in the **MIDDLE OF WINTER** while she chit-chatted with her suffragette friends, you could very well have frozen to death.

I don't think that would look very good for the Women's Social and Political Union.[2] Imagine the headline:

GIRL, AGED ELEVEN, MEETS A FROSTY END OUTSIDE WSPU HEADQUARTERS!

WSPU HQ

VOTES FOR WOMEN

I had such a jolly time talking with you! Do you often go to WSPU events? My sister, Sarah, is becoming quite the radical.[3]

2 In 1913 women were not allowed to vote. The Women's Social and Political Union (WSPU) – nicknamed 'the suffragettes' – was an organization led by Emmeline Pankhurst campaigning for women to be granted the same rights to vote as men.
3 A radical is a person who wants to change the way things are done in society.

She's always dragging me along so she can learn more about the WSPU. Mother can't bear it. Usually Sarah takes me to the Kensington branch.

"I'm just taking Mary for a walk around Kensington Gardens," she'll call to Mother and Father as she pulls me out the door, but we always end up at the WSPU headquarters or at the WSPU shop where she meets with her friends and picks up a copy of *The Suffragette*.[4] There are **HARDLY EVER** any girls my age around for me to talk to, so I end up sitting like a Freda-no-friends and doodling in my sketchbook. I was thrilled to hear that you like to draw too! Please send me one of your pictures! I love drawing all sorts of things. This is our cat, Milly. We named her after Millicent Fawcett:[5]

Millicent Fawcett

---

4 The Women's Social and Political Union's official magazine. Each issue contained news, letters from the WSPU leader, Emmeline Pankhurst, to her supporters and information about upcoming events.
5 The leader of the National Union of Women's Suffrage Societies (NUWSS), Millicent Fawcett believed women could achieve the vote using non-violent campaigning.

And I love drawing things from my imagination, like me as 'Detective Inspector M. Forrest':

Father thinks I could be a cartoonist when I grow up, but I want to be a **GREAT DETECTIVE** like Sherlock Holmes and solve **GRUESOME MURDERS**.

Have you ever tried drawing funny pictures? I **LOVE** drawing them. They make me feel much better when I'm grumpy!

Like this picture of my brother, Edward. He and I went for a walk in Hyde Park this morning. He wouldn't stop chasing the poor pigeons off the path.

They didn't **REALLLLLY** attack him like in my picture, but I wish they had. That would teach him!

I asked Mother if I could write to you and she thought it would be a wonderful way to practise my handwriting. She said young women need to stick together. **HAHA!** I've put my address at the top of the letter. I hope you write back soon! It would be lovely to meet up properly one day, too.

Yours,

Mary Forrest

P.S. Are you a suffragette?

Christine Sedgwick
3 Stoneheath Place
Marylebone
London

6th January 1913

Dear Mary,

Thank you so much for your letter! I was really hoping you would write! I had great fun talking to you, too. So much better than counting the grimy pigeons outside in the cold. I was starting to wish I was a grimy pigeon myself, then at least I could puff up my feathers to keep warm. Though not if your brother was going to chase me away!

Jane wasn't angry at all! Her face always looks a bit like that. I overheard mother telling her off the other day.

"Do practise softening your expression," Mother said. "You really should smile more, or, dare I say, laugh once in a while?"

"Why on earth would I want to do that?" Jane asked. Mother told her that no man wants to marry a grump and that frowning will give you wrinkles.

And Jane just frowned even more!

Jane is actually my cousin, not my sister. Though people say we look very alike, even though she's eighteen and I'm eleven. I don't think I look quite as grumpy. Jane has lived with us ever since her mother died. She has been acting as a kind of governess to me.

I think she only meant to pop in to the WSPU meeting for a moment yesterday, but got caught up in the latest news! She doesn't often leave me to freeze outside.

We did make it home for dinner, but I didn't have time to change, which annoyed Father. He likes me to look tidy at the table.[6] He doesn't seem to mind when my brother, Charles, tumbles in after digging through the leaf pile in the garden. Last Friday, Charles interrupted our soup by plopping a bird's nest onto the table! It was hopping with fleas!

"It's important for a young man to be curious," Father said, as fleas jumped all over our dinner. I wouldn't like to see Father's face if I came in like that.

Your sketches are **SHOCKING!**[7] They made me laugh so hard I had to pretend I was having a coughing fit. Only I was a bit too good at pretending and Mother tried to give

---

6 In 1913 wealthy families like Christine's would change into their fancier clothes for dinner.
7 Christine makes a good point. Girls weren't known for drawing very funny pictures in 1913. Girls like Christine and Mary would have been expected to spend their time doing needlework, learning how to make polite conversation and how to keep a home nice and clean for a husband.

me some of the horrid medicine Doctor Percival gave me the last time I had the flu.

This is my first ever funny picture:

I usually prefer to sketch flowers from the garden or to copy birds from some of the natural history books Father buys for Charles. I love to do needlework too. Sometimes I try to sew some of the pictures I have drawn. My mother is wonderful at needlework. Jane is utterly dreadful at it. She always pricks her fingers and gets ever so angry. Here is a flower I stitched:

It would be wonderful to meet again, but I'm afraid Father can be difficult about who I spend time with. **BORING!** So I think for now we might have to make do with writing to each other. I don't get many letters, so that will be exciting. If Jane sneaks off to a WSPU meeting on one of our outings again, perhaps I will bump into you!

Very best wishes,
Christine Sedgwick

P.S. I am not a suffragette, I don't think, though I suspect Jane is. My mother certainly isn't. Are you? I'm not sure that I know what one is.

12th January 1913

Dear Christine,

Oh my goodness! That flower is **AMAZING**. It's a pansy, isn't it? I **LOVE** the colours. Purple, white and green![8] Very radical, maybe you *are* a suffragette.

A **SUFFRAGETTE** is someone who wants women to be able to vote in elections. They believe it's unfair that only men can vote and that they should not have to obey laws they have no say in making. Sarah says that's why suffragettes are prepared to **BREAK THE LAW** in protest at not being allowed to vote. You've probably heard about them smashing windows? I'm not a suffragette **YET**, but I do think it is **TOTALLY UNFAIR** that women aren't allowed to vote. Don't you? When you see all the completely silly things that men do, it seems incredible that they have been in charge of everything for so long!

8 The colours of the WSPU were purple meaning dignity, white meaning purity and green meaning hope.

Ridiculous things men do:

- Declare war on people
- Play golf
- Grow enormous twirly moustaches
- Go Morris dancing[9]

...I could go on, but I don't think I need to!

I think I would like to be a suffragette when I grow up. That is, if women don't already have the vote by then. **HAHA!**

Mother and Father are **SUFFRAGISTS** and think that is very important that I know the difference.

Mother is a member of the National Union of Women's Suffrage Societies.[10] The NUWSS are determined to achieve the vote **PEACEFULLY**, without breaking the law - or **WINDOWS**.

The NUWSS use peaceful petitions[11] and campaigning. They want to work **WITH** politicians rather than **AGAINST** them. It's all just lots of talking and hosting tea parties, if you ask me.

Do take a scone, Prime Minister. Oh, and please may we have the vote?

---

9 An English folk dance performed in a group. Men dance with sticks, handkerchiefs and bells.
10 An organization made up of groups of suffragists from all over the country, who all wanted women to have the vote.
11 A letter signed by lots of people demanding change.

SUFFRAGETTE

No men allowed in WSPU

Led by Emmeline Pankhurst

Can be law breakers!

VOTES FOR WOMEN

WSPU

Want women to be able to vote on the same terms as men (must own property and be over thirty)

SUFFRAGIST

VOTES FOR WOMEN

NUWSS

Led by Millicent Fawcett

Don't break the law

Want all men and women to vote

Sarah is becoming a suffragette. Mother **HATES** it, but they don't talk about in front of me. I HATE BEING ELEVEN SOMETIMES!

My sister says the suffragette's leader, Mrs Pankhurst, kicks people out if they don't agree with her. THE MEANY! She said Mrs Pankhurst sees the WSPU as an army and its members as soldiers. Sarah said wars would never be won if armies stopped to vote on what to do all the time. It's better if they just do what they're told.

Perhaps she has a point.

Mother has always worked for the NUWSS, organizing events and supporting political parties that favour women getting the vote. But Sarah says all the hours of work Mother and her friends have put in have **ACHIEVED NOTHING**. Politicians have come for dinner and drunk lots of cups of tea with Mother and Father and made all sorts of **PROMISES** but **NOTHING** has changed. WOMEN *STILL* CANNOT VOTE. Sarah says that if the NUWSS way of doing things worked, women would have had the vote ages ago.

Sarah wants to be a suffragette because she believes that **NOW** is the time for action. "**DEEDS NOT WORDS**," as Mrs Pankhurst would say.[12]

"Mrs Pankhurst is determined to bring change quickly," Sarah told me. She showed me a letter, signed by Emmeline Pankhurst herself! It looked quite crinkled, as if Sarah has read it lots of times.

"The letter is about a debate that's going to happen in Parliament – about women's voting rights," Sarah said. Apparently, on 20th January they're going to talk about women's right to vote again. But Sarah told me not to get my hopes up. She says they've discussed it lots of times before and nothing has changed.

Gloomy old Sarah, my hopes ARE up, whatever she says. Fingers and toes crossed <u>**SOMETHING**</u> changes.

Write soon!

Mary

---

12 'Deeds not words' was one of the slogans of the WSPU. It means it is more important to do something to make a change, rather than just talking about it.

15th January 1913

Dear Mary,

My mother is certainly not a suffragist. She has said many times that she does not want the vote. When I asked her why, she folded her arms and frowned.

"A man's place is out in the public and a woman's place is with her family and her home," she said. "It isn't right that women should get to vote. Women do not fight in armies so why should they be involved in sending them to war? Women do not work in coal mines or as builders, so why should they get a say in working rights? It is God's will that men and women are important in different spheres."

Don't ask me what she means by 'spheres', I don't have a clue! It made me think of men and women floating around in big bubbles full of all the things they are supposed to be interested in...

"Your mother is quite right," Father said. "It is **UNNATURAL** for a woman to vote!"

He often says things like that. He read out a story from the newspaper this morning, about women setting fire to postboxes.

He thinks that if the suffragettes carry on like this, it only goes to prove that women aren't sensible enough to vote. He always looks like he has smelled something nasty when he says the word "suffragette". The suffragettes better not set fire to our postbox. I would be heartbroken to miss one of your letters!

Father thinks that if women get the vote, soon we'll have woman police officers, judges, soldiers... Can you imagine? Who would look after the home? Who would take care of the children? I know I wouldn't like Mother to be out all day voting and fighting wars. I would miss her horribly.

I'm not sure I completely agree with my parents but I do see how women are more suited to life in the home. We have children, after all. Father wouldn't have the **FIRST IDEA** how to cook a meal or mend our clothes.

Jane is always very quiet when my parents are talking about this. Her mother (my aunt) felt very differently. I think she was a suffragette or perhaps a suffragist, I'm not sure, but I remember her and my father having arguments about it. Well, they did before she got ill and died. Jane probably gets her ideas from her mother.

Very best wishes,
Christine

P.S. I'm glad you liked my flower. Jane brought the thread home for me the other day. I thought they were just pretty colours. **HAHA**, as you would say.

30th January 1913

Dear Christine,

SURPRISE, SURPRISE, that bill that would have given women the vote did not make it through Parliament, did you hear? I am so disappointed! The Speaker of the House of Commons said it would have to be raised as a **WHOLE NEW BILL**, not just tacked on the end of a men's reform bill, as it was a different thing altogether. Which means they have to start **ALL OVER AGAIN**. Mother was **FURIOUS**. She said she'd hoped for more for her girls.

Father held Mother and said they would fight on together. My father can be wonderful sometimes. Sarah rushed out as soon as she heard. I am sure she went to see her friends at the WSPU. Mother was even more upset than she had been last year when the bill before this one failed. Father says she will be back to her old self in no time, giving out handbills,[13] hosting lunches and whatnot. I know he is right, but I hate seeing her so unhappy. Sarah said that Mrs Pankhurst asked

---

13 An old-fashioned word for leaflets.

the suffragettes to be ready to 'be militant', which basically means to smash and burn things if the bill didn't go through. And now it hasn't...

It feels funny to be so upset, myself. It's not as if I could have voted for a long time anyway.[14] How did Jane take the news?

Yours,
Mary

P.S. I spotted this AWFUL picture in one of mother's magazines. I mean, really... Perhaps your father might like it? Ha.

---

14 If the bill had passed, it would have given the right to vote to women who were over 25 years old and owned property, or were married to someone who owned property.

13th February 1913

Dear Mary,

I can't say I know how Jane felt about the failed bill, but she has been acting even more strangely than normal. She usually takes my lessons very seriously, but this week I've been left on my own a lot, which is great because I get to draw. She calls it 'independent study' but I feel sure she's been up to something. And then, last night, a very odd thing happened...

I don't know what to make of it. The clock on the landing had just struck midnight. **BONG!** I heard a creaking on the stairs and sneaked out of bed on my tippiest of tippy-toes to investigate. I wondered if it was our maid, Martha, doing some late-night cleaning. But when I peeked out I saw it was Jane, in her overcoat, on her way down the stairs.

The click of my door opening must have startled her, because she froze. I had the brilliant idea of squeaking loudly, so that Jane would think it was just a little mouse that she had heard. What I'd forgotten though, was that Jane is **ABSOLUTELY TERRIFIED** of all scuttling, scampering things and therefore jumped a clear foot off the floor. We both waited for **aaages** before she finally carried on down the stairs, her eyes darting all around for anything scuttling. Whoops! I heard the front door open and close and I ran to my window to see Jane with two other women who must have been waiting outside. They hurried off down the street towards the park. Jane's friends were each carrying something bulky but I couldn't see what it was. I went back to bed but lay awake until I heard the front door open again. I creeped back to my bedroom door and peered out. When Jane came up the stairs, she looked **flushed** and **wild-eyed** and had a black smudge on her cheek.

I can't speak to Mother about it, as I'm frightened that Father would **HIT THE ROOF** if he found out about her sneaking out, and I can't ask Jane in case she thinks I have been snooping. She is very private and gets most **vexed**[15] if she thinks Charles or I have been into her room. Where do you think she could have been? Did you notice anything odd about Sarah last night? Could she have sneaked out too? I just don't know what to do.

Yours,
Christine

---

15 Really angry.

Dear Christine,

That's quite the mystery you have described there. Perhaps a case for Detective Inspector M. Forrest herself! Sarah's room is right next to mine so I know she didn't sneak out that night. She snores dreadfully and I would have noticed the peace and quiet.

Do you think Jane was headed to Regent's Park? Also, do you think the women could have been carrying cans? You know, the kind that contain petrol. There was an attack that very night on the Regent's Park snack kiosk. Somebody **SET IT ALIGHT**! According to the paper, whoever did it scraped '**VOTES FOR WOMEN**' into the path and left a couple of petrol cans behind. I hope to goodness Jane wasn't involved. She could get into an **AWFUL** lot of trouble, and I don't mean go-to-your-room-now-young-lady trouble, but grown-up **GET-ARRESTED-AND-GO-TO-PRISON TROUBLE**.

I would suggest you destroy this letter as soon as you have read it. I would hate your mother or father to see it. I burned your letter in the fire in my grate just before writing this one!

Yours,
Mary Forrest, Detective Inspector

P.S. I didn't think Jane would be so silly as to be scared of a tiny little mouse! **HAHA!**

16th February 1913

Dear Mary,

I did as you said with your letter. I think you are right. This is most definitely a case for Detective M. Forrest and I will therefore refer to what happened from now on as the **CASE OF THE MIDNIGHT SNACK.**

I can't think of any other reason for Jane to be out at that time of night, other than to go for a midnight snack in Regent's Park. What do you think I should do now? Should I ask her? She must know that Father would not let her live with us if he knew. Mother loves Jane dearly; she promised my aunt that she would take care of her, but in this house what Father says goes and I don't think I have ever seen Mother stand in his way.

How could Jane take such a big risk sneaking out like that? If I saw her sneak out, anyone could have. Do you think you could ask Sarah what she thinks I should do? I'm so worried. Jane is like a sister to me. A very annoying and superior sister, but a sister all the same, and I would hate for anything to happen to her.

Yours,
Christine

17th February 1913

Dear Christine,

Just a quick letter about the **CASE OF THE MIDNIGHT SNACK**. I spoke to Sarah about what we suspect. Don't worry I made her swear not to tell ANYONE! And Sarah is a pretty good secret keeper, especially since I know how much time she spends at WSPU headquarters. Sarah says you should let Jane know you saw her sneak out, but not that you suspect anything. It will let her know that she needs to be more careful. Sarah says that Jane does need to be VERY CAREFUL. They've come to know each other rather well recently.

"She's lovely, but I think she might be a bit of a 'YOUNG HOT BLOOD'," Sarah said. I asked her what that meant. She told me it's what the WSPU call some of the younger members who go out of their way to put themselves in real danger for the cause.

One thing's for sure, it doesn't suggest someone who gets the vapours[16] at the sight of a little mouse!

Speak to Jane and try not to worry. Once she knows you spotted her sneaking out for a 'midnight snack', I'm sure she won't be tempted to again, for a short while at least.

Very best wishes,
Mary Forrest, D.I.

16 A sudden feeling of faintness.

Dear Mary,

I spoke to Jane about her 'midnight snack' during our walk today. As soon as I mentioned it, her face went as white as a sheet.

"Have you been spying on me? Did your mother or father see me leave? Did you tell them?" she asked, taking me by the shoulders and shaking me.

"No, I haven't; no, they didn't; and no, of course not. As if I would!" I replied, offended. Ugh! I think she is more scared of being caught by Father than by the police.

"I did tell my best friend, Mary," I said. "But she's a brilliant secret keeper!" I pointed out that I was worried she would think that I had been spying on her (which she did) and that I was scared she would get really, really angry with me (which she was).

"I needed to tell SOMEONE or I would have exploded!" I said. "And Mary would never tell ANYONE."

I'd like to say that she then apologized and admitted

that I was right, but I cannot say that because she did **NOT** do that. Instead she pulled that face Mother pulls at Father when it looks like she wants to scream at him and doesn't. The one where her lips disappear and turn into a thin white line.

I was going to leave it at that, but then she asked where I thought she went. I told her about our investigation into the **CASE OF THE MIDNIGHT SNACK**. She said you and I must be quite the detectives! Can you believe we cracked our first case on our very first attempt? We really should think about becoming real-life detectives! Though, I don't think Father would like that.

I told her I was scared for her and I didn't understand why she was doing it. I argued that women, like Mother and maybe myself, did not want the vote. That we thought Father would vote for us, so we didn't need to vote, too.

"Who will vote in my interests? Your father?" Jane said. "If you do not marry, will Charles vote for you? For both of us? You are much cleverer than Charles. Don't you think that is unfair? What about men with bad morals or who aren't as clever as you or I? Do they think of us when they vote?"

Now, don't these fine fellows look like sensible voters?

I'm not sure I fully see her point, but she is right that I am much cleverer than Charles. HE IS AN <u>IDIOT!</u> AND <u>MEAN!</u> I suppose I see what she is saying about Father not really voting with her wishes in mind. They don't agree on anything. And Charles?! He doesn't do anything that isn't selfish.

Jane kissed me and promised that she would be more careful. She did confirm one of my worries though. She would rather be arrested than face another of Father's lectures.

Do write soon!
Christine

Dear Christine,

Well, I suppose Jane took the news as well as could be expected! SURELY YOU MUST AGREE that it's silly that nasty, cruel and selfish people can vote just because they are MEN.

Did you see the picture in the paper of Lloyd George's house?[17] They say suffragettes SET IT ON FIRE. Can you believe it? An actual house. I call that some nerve. Walton-on-the-Heath isn't far from my Aunt Violet's house in Surrey. Aunt Violet said the police suspect that Mrs Pankhurst did it herself! I can't imagine she would do something like that, can you?

Mother doesn't think it matters whether she struck the match or not. Mother wants the vote every bit as much as Mrs Pankhurst, but she thinks there are more sensible ways of going about it.

"Mrs Pankhurst as good as did it by telling her suffragettes to commit violent acts!" Mother said. Mother thinks that burning down houses brings the wrong type of attention to the cause.

"Attention is attention," Sarah said, "and this fire got the WSPU on the front page."

17 The Chancellor of the Exchequer at the time.

Sarah said that the WSPU is an organization for women who are tired of being ignored. And after the failed bill last month, she's sure we'll see much more of the same. Mother looked like she was really going to lose her temper, but then she

The NUWSS is for women who want to be taken seriousy!

There are few things as serious as a house on fire!

just sighed and said that she hoped that Sarah would never think of doing anything more than talk so wildly.

"Don't worry, I'm not going to set fire to any buildings," said Sarah. "But I wouldn't speak ill of any of the brave women that do."

I **HATE** it when they argue. Father says it is Mother's fault for insisting they raise daughters with opinions, which made us all laugh. Thank goodness, because it was all getting very serious and awkward! I agree with Sarah: there is only one thing worse than being talked about and that is not being talked about. Lloyd George's burning house has got people talking even if they don't like what is being said.

Do write soon!

Mary

Dear Mary,

Yes, the pictures of Lloyd George's house really did get everyone talking. Father can barely talk about anything else!

"I can't understand how the men in the families of these 'beasts' can show themselves in public," he said when he saw the news in the paper. "It is a man's job to make sure women don't bring shame on the family." I said quietly that perhaps the fathers of the ladies who committed the crime were dead so there was no one to stop them. "Well, I hope that when I die, Charles will make sure that no one in this family behaves in such a shocking way!" Father said. Charles smirked and I had to hold on to my leg to stop myself from kicking him under the table. Again - Charles!? If anyone were to bring shame on the family it would <u>be</u> Charles! He said if these women weren't stopped, someone was going to get killed and 'that Pankhurst woman', as he calls her, would have blood on her hands.

Jane replied that Mrs Pankhurst had given orders that WSPU members were only to hurt property and not people, and that human life was sacred.

"Mrs Pankhurst is a fool if she thinks she can run her rabble of wild women like an army. It would be easier to herd cats," Father said.

"Are you saying women are no better than animals?" Jane asked angrily.

"These ones aren't. These women are behaving like animals," Father replied.[18]

I hope Jane would never do anything so dangerous, but as Father spoke she had a look on her face that suggested she was ready to burn down the very house we were standing in.

I don't think that Mrs Pankhurst struck the match herself. She has so many followers to do this for her, I don't see why she would have to.

Yours truly,
Christine

18 People who were against women getting the vote often compared women to animals saying lovely things such as, "If a woman can vote, why not a horse?"

Dear Christine,

I SAW HER! Mrs Pankhurst! Yesterday morning Sarah came running up the stairs and burst in my room (WITHOUT KNOCKING, I may add). I WAS ABOUT to give Sarah a lecture about RESPECTING MY PRIVACY when she grabbed hold of my arm.

"You MUST come with me, AT ONCE," she said dramatically. "You won't regret it."

I rolled my eyes so she could see I was not impressed. Sarah always thinks everything she does is **EXCITING** and **IMPORTANT**. It is very annoying having an older sister sometimes, I hope your cousin treats you with a little more respect. I bet she doesn't though. UGH! I am losing my point. Sorry!

She dragged me to Chelsea Town Hall. We jostled our way through the crowd and squashed into the corner of the room. From there we craned our heads toward the stage to see above all the hats. Sarah whispered that she thought we were just in time. Just after we got our spot someone, came out onto the stage and introduced Mrs Pankhurst. I have to admit, that was quite exciting and I was glad Sarah had made me come along.

Oh Christine, Mrs Pankhurst was **MAGNIFICENT**. Such a brave and powerful speaker. I have never seen a woman stand up in public and address a crowd the way she did. It was as though she were a man.[19] I can see what Sarah and Jane see in her and her cause after listening to her.

She compared the fight of the WSPU with that of Oliver Cromwell and his men during the Civil War.[20] I just learned a little about that from my governess. I'd never thought about the campaign for the right to vote being like a war before! I wish you had been there, Christine. I was so stirred up after hearing her that I felt like I wanted to rush outside and smash something myself.

19 Women in 1913 were not expected to speak in public, let alone be good at it.
20 The English Civil war was fought in 1642. One side believed that King Charles I should be able to rule without Parliament and the other side, led by Oliver Cromwell, believed that the king needed Parliament's permission to rule. Oliver Cromwell's side won and in 1649 King Charles I had his head chopped off.

Sarah and I tried to remember our favourite parts of her speech on the walk home. I liked a part about how brave men fought against the king in the Civil War. The king believed God had given him the right to rule, so it went TOTALLY AGAINST the way things were done for the people to fight against him. But they did it anyway!

"I liked that bit too!" Sarah said. "And when Mrs Pankhurst went on to say that our fight, the fight for women to be allowed to vote, is even harder, because instead of one ruler, women today are fighting eight million men who believe God gave them the right to be in charge. Ha!"

Oh, Christine, I do hope you get to see her speak one day. She isn't the **DANGEROUS** 'monster' the newspapers (and I'm sure your father) says she is. She is an **INTELLIGENT** and **COURAGEOUS** woman who wants to change the world. I suppose that does make her a **LITTLE** dangerous. **HAHA.**

Yours excitedly,
Mary Forrest, Suffragette (haha)

P.S. Mrs Pankhurst said she's going to say she started the fire at Lloyd George's, even though I'm sure she didn't. I don't know if she is brave or crazy. Perhaps she is **BOTH.** I don't think I could ever believe in anything enough to go to prison for something I didn't do.

Dear Mary,

Oh, Mary, that does sound very exciting. I'm not sure how I feel about the WSPU, but I would very much like to see Mrs Pankhurst speak. Father took us all to see Lord Curzon[21] speak at an anti-suffrage rally at the Royal Albert Hall last year. He is against women having the vote. Needless to say, Jane stayed home. She would have hated it! Lord Curzon sounded a lot like Father, only louder and he was surrounded by a lot more people that agreed with him. He was saying that women did not have calm enough minds to vote. Which I thought was funny because mother is always a lot calmer than Father about practically everything. In fact, I can't think of many things Father is calm about, except golf and... No, I can't think of anything else. Father is a friend of Lord Curzon and has played golf at his course. He was a great speaker too, though I am sure what they spoke about was quite different!

I can't believe Mrs Pankhurst is going to take the blame

21 Lord Curzon was president of the National League for Opposing Women's Suffrage. As former Viceroy of India (ruler on behalf of the British Crown), he believed allowing women to vote would damage the British Empire.

for the fire! I would never want to go to prison. Jane has told me stories of how her friends have been treated. I am so worried that Jane is going to end up in prison... She's proved that she's a bit wild with the **CASE OF THE MIDNIGHT SNACK.** My aunt had wanted Jane to continue her education and become a teacher. But when Mother and Father took her in, Father said it would be better for Jane to find a husband.

"If Jane is so fond of teaching, let her earn her keep as Christine's governess," Father said one evening, not long after my aunt had died. And that was that.

"Now I have lost my mother AND my future," Jane told me. "I have nothing left to lose."

I am so frightened for her and for myself. I would hate something bad to happen to her. I wish she would settle down and do as Father says.

Yours truly,
Christine

1st March 1913

Dear Christine,

Poor Jane! She's been through so much. I do hope she doesn't do anything against the law... Prison does sound awful! Sarah talks about how horrible prison is for suffragettes, too.

"Lots of women go on hunger strike," she told me, "because they want to be treated like political prisoners rather than common criminals." I wasn't sure there was a difference, but Sarah said there is a **BIG** difference. By not letting the women be political prisoners, the government are telling the people that 'votes for women' is not something that is important to them. Also, political prisoners are allowed to talk to one another and wear their own clothes, rather than prison clothes that are really scratchy and horrible. So the women are protesting by not eating anything.

"The government is terrified one of the prisoners will starve themselves to death, then people will be so angry they will vote against them," Sarah told me.

I asked if the women got terribly ill. My tummy was

rumbling at the very thought of stopping eating, even for a day!

"Some do. And sometimes, they are force-fed," Sarah said. Imagine! It didn't seem possible to me, not in Great Britain, but when we got home Sarah showed me a leaflet with a picture of a woman being held in a chair. A gentleman is pouring something into a funnel attached to a tube that disappears into the woman's nose. I was sure she was just trying to frighten me, but she told me that it happens every day.[22] Imagine being forced to eat ... **THROUGH YOUR NOSE**! It looked like very cruel torture. I felt quite sick.

Sarah doesn't think they'll force-feed Mrs Pankhurst though. She says it is mainly lower-class women who experience this in prison. It's terrible, isn't it?

All this horrible news. Perhaps being eleven isn't the worst thing in the world. No ... wait ... it definitely is. At least grown-ups can try and do something about it. Do you have any funny stories to cheer me up?

Yours truly,
Mary

---

22 It was common for women who went on hunger strike to be force-fed. Not only was it unpleasant, it was also dangerous.

Dear Mary,

I do! I do! I do have a funny story. And you know better than anyone that NOTHING FUNNY ever happens in this house. I had to write as soon as it happened! We have a **JOKER** in our house. And you will never guess who. None other than **JANE** herself, if you can believe it. Jane is usually so serious, but today she played the most wonderful joke on Father. After breakfast, Father folded up his newspaper and took it with him to the water closet,[23] as is his horrible habit. Yuck! Moments later he came out almost foaming at the mouth with rage. He stormed past me and flatly refused to tell me what was the matter.

When I asked what had happened, Mother told me that someone had swapped the soap with 'Votes for Women' soap. I rushed to the water closet, and there it was! Look, I've sent you the wrapper. Isn't that too much? I was shocked, but not for the reason Mother and Father were, rather because I didn't know Jane had such a wonderful joke in her! What next, WSPU toilet paper?

23 A polite word for the toilet.

Father told Mother to have a stern word with Martha, but Mother said it must have been some sort of mistake.

"Martha is a huge fan of a bargain. Perhaps the soap was on special offer!" Mother said. She told Father she would make sure Martha didn't do it again. Mother must have known it was Jane though and I know for **A FACT** that she didn't speak to Martha about it. I asked Jane about it on our walk and she gave me a little wink. Ha!

Very best wishes,
Christine

17th March 1913

Dear Christine,

HAHA! Your letter made me laugh out loud! What a wonderful joke. I would have liked to have seen your father's face. Isn't your mother a dark horse for not letting on? Well done, I say!

I've seen suffragette soap. You can get all kinds of 'Votes for Women' things in shops nowadays, from buttons that cost a penny to very fancy and expensive silk gowns. Mother and Sarah think it is an excellent way to raise funds for the cause. Father says it is a great way for department stores to make piles of money while protecting their shop windows.

WELL DONE, Jane, I say! It was lovely to have a jolly good giggle with all the dark news.

My aunt wrote to say that the suffragettes had set fire to a house in Cheam, which isn't far from her. No one was hurt of course, but I'm sure it's only a matter of time. How can the suffragettes be sure no one is home?

Mrs Pankhurst has said more than once that human life is sacred and that the WSPU will only target empty houses. But surely there will be some accident if this carries on?

Even Father is starting to get a bit cheesed off. He has had to cancel more than one game of golf this year. He is a member of a club in Richmond. He said the groundsmen are having awful bother with suffragettes vandalising the course. They keep digging up the nice smooth greens! The Prime Minister is a member there, so father thinks the suffragettes are targeting the course to get his attention. The club is doing everything they can to protect the lawns. The staff take turns to guard them overnight with torches. Imagine having to stay up all night to guard grass! Sounds like the one thing more boring than listening to Father talk about golf.

He said he knows Mrs Pankhurst wanted to stir people up, but did she have to stir up his favourite golf course?

Sarah said that was rather the point. **HAHA!**

   I don't suppose Jane has been out for any more MIDNIGHT SNACKS near golf courses?

Yours truly,

Mary

Dear Mary,

No midnight snacks here. Jane has been on her best behaviour since the **CASE OF THE GREAT SOAP SWITCHEROO**. She has put a lot of work into our lessons and is even giving me extra lessons on the piano. She taught me a marvellous song:

Shout, shout, up with your song!

March, march, swing you along,

Cry with the wind, for the dawn is breaking,

Wide blows our banner, and hope is waking.

Song with its story, dreams with their glory,

Lo! they call, and glad is their word!

Louder and louder it swells!

Thunder of freedom, the voice of the Lord!

Do you know it? It really stirs you up when you sing it with gusto. Father says he has never heard me play so well.

I don't agree with suffragettes burning down people's houses, but I think golf courses are an excellent target. What better way to get the politicians' attention than by spoiling their fun? Father likes to play golf, too. Mother used to play a lot when she was growing up in Scotland but doesn't get to so much now. Also, there are so many rules about when women can play and where they are allowed to go at most courses that she says it hardly seems worth going.[27]

Very best wishes,
Christine

P.S. Sorry for my slow reply. We went away for Easter, to the seaside at Great Yarmouth. My mother wanted to 'take some air.' The air we took was rather too cold for my liking, and smelled of seaweed... But I did make some rather good sandcastles and we had lots of delicious ice cream. I wish I could have saved some for you!

---

24 Some golf clubs in the United Kingdom still restrict the times when female members are allowed to play or ban women from going into certain areas. Muirfield Golf Club in Scotland didn't allow women to become members until March 2017.

Dear Christine,

Mrs Pankhurst is going to prison. THREE WHOLE YEARS. It seems like a very long sentence, especially as she didn't set fire to Lloyd George's house herself. It was **SO BRAVE** of her to take the blame. I can't imagine being away from my family for three years.

I asked Sarah what the WSPU would do without Mrs Pankhurst. "Her daughter Christabel will be in charge," Sarah said. "And if Christabel is arrested, there are many other women that would take her place. This movement isn't about ONE woman but about ALL women."

That made me think of when I heard Mrs Pankhurst speak in Chelsea Town Hall. She said that if "one falls down by the way, a hundred will rise to take her place." Imagine that, a hundred Mrs Pankhursts! That would be enough to give your father nightmares! **HAHA!**

On the subject of nightmares, I was thinking about

Mrs Pankhurst. Prison is bad enough, but what if she goes on hunger strike? Nobody can survive three years without food. Perhaps they will have to force-feed Mrs Pankhurst after all. I brought it up at the dinner table yesterday.

"The dining table is no place for this kind of talk," Mother said.

"...But I'm talking about food," I said.

Sarah said that the government have passed a new law. Now, instead of being force-fed, a prisoner who is on hunger strike can be released until they have recovered enough to finish their prison sentence.

"Oh, that's jolly kind of them!" I said.

But Sarah scoffed. "Kind? The Cat and Mouse Act?"[25]

She told me the government are releasing very ill prisoners to be looked after at home. Then as soon as the women are a bit better, they're hauled **BACK TO PRISON** by the police.

Our cat, Milly, does this when she brings mice into the kitchen, she catches and releases the poor animal again and again, like a cruel game. If father is home when it happens, he takes the poor mouse away from naughty Milly and sets it free in the garden. He says it is cruel to watch an animal suffer. The government seem happy to watch women suffer.

25 The Cat and Mouse Act, properly known as the Prisoners (Temporary Discharge for Ill Health) Bill, was passed on 25th March and became law in April.

Father says the government are scared that the outcry over force-feeding prisoners will lose them votes in the next election, so that's why they've come up with this new rule. And can you **BELIEVE** it? The Cat and Mouse Act was proposed at the beginning of this month and is **ALREADY** a law. **WHOOSH**! Just like that.

"It does show how quickly the government can move when they want to," Father said, sadly. Giving votes to women isn't as URGENT as being able to TORTURE them.

Yours truly,

Mary

P.S. Don't be so sure about Jane being on her best behaviour!
I do know that song, it is a favourite of the WSPU. They sing
it on all their marches. Look, Sarah has the sheet music. It's
even called 'The March of the Women'!

I am glad your father enjoys it. I promise I will bring you
A WHOLE BAG OF SUGARED ALMONDS the next time I see
you if you manage to get him to sing along! **I DARE YOU!**
I underestimated your cousin, she is a comic genius! Haha!

THE MARCH OF THE WOMEN.

Ethel Smyth, Mus.Doc.

Dear Mary,

That sounds awful! And more bad news, the WSPU headquarters were raided by the police yesterday. Jane took me to Kingsway as soon as she saw it in the paper. She wanted to go alone, but I've been watching her like a hawk lately. I was really sneaky and asked, in front of Mother, if I could go with her to the park to sketch the roses. I have been struggling with roses and I felt sure Mother would tell Jane to take me with her so I could practise.

Police officers never struck me as untidy people, with their well-pressed uniforms and everything, but they had made an awful mess. It was an absolute PIGSTY! Apparently, the police had taken piles upon piles of papers away with them. Lists of members, receipts and such. I can't think what they could want with it all. With all the blowing up of postboxes and burning down of buildings in the papers every morning, surely they should be looking for matches and petrol cans, not receipts for packets of biscuits?

As we were helping to clear up, Jane said the police are really cracking down on the WSPU now. They want to silence them for ever. Members are no longer allowed to hold rallies in parks and the police have contacted the owners of halls where meetings are held and told them they are not allowed to let the suffragettes hire out their rooms.

I can't see what the WSPU will do now. Most of their leaders are in prison or are waiting to go on trial. Their offices have been raided. The police even arrested and charged the printer of *The Suffragette* and so there will be no more issues of the magazine. Jane was quiet on the way home. She must know all is lost. I hope this means she will settle down.

Yours truly,
Christine

P.S. You can keep your sugared almonds! If Father knew his new favourite ditty was all the rage at suffragette sing-a-longs, he'd have Jane sharing a cell with Mrs Pankhurst before you could shout 'Hark!'.

P.P.S. What do you think of this rose? I think there is something off about it, but I can't work out what.

13th May 1913

Dear Christine,

That rose is beautiful! It looks **PERFECT** to me. I love how you always manage to get so much detail into your drawings. If you weren't my best friend I would be horribly jealous of your talent. Haha! I'm dreadful at drawing flowers.

Sarah told me about the offices. I think the police took the papers to help them hunt down members of the WSPU and readers of the magazine. They want to know **ALL** of the names and addresses of anyone who has anything to do with it, whether they're people who supply them with biscuits or people who set fire to postboxes. I think the police want to know this information so they can **THREATEN** these people and charge them with **CRIMES**.

It won't work though. Putting Mrs Pankhurst in prison has only made WSPU members more active. They've disturbed a wasps' nest and now the wasps are buzzing around stinging everybody and driving them crazy. They may have trapped a few in a jar, but when they get out they are only going to be angrier. **BUZZ, BUZZ!**

Did you see this morning, an explosive machine was found in St Paul's Cathedral?[26] And it's not just in London. All over the country, boathouses and train stations are burning. Anywhere suffragettes can cause chaos without hurting anyone. The government are desperate to stop it, but they don't stand a chance.

I would keep your eye on Jane. There are a lot of people going out for midnight snacks at the moment. Sarah thinks this will get worse before it gets better.

But in happier news, I am going to stay with my aunt for the Derby next month! I hope Mother lets me wear a longer dress, like the kind she and Sarah wear. I would love to go to the Derby in a long skirt and parasol. I think I would look lovely, but I am sure mother will find some sort of babyish sailor dress. She says we will each get something new, but I hardly see the point if it's going to be the usual little girls' clothes.[27]

Sarah says I should be in no hurry to wear a corset. She says you can't run or climb in them and she's sure they must have been designed by men to keep women from trying to do anything fun or interesting. I think she looks **VERY ELEGANT** and that I would too.

26 The suffragettes targeted churches because Church leaders wouldn't choose a side on whether women should have the vote or not, preferring to keep out of it. To the suffragettes, not speaking up for them meant the Church was against them.
27 In 1913, girls did not wear long dresses and corsets until their late teens.

I would like to go to the
Derby dressed like this.

I will almost certainly be
going dressed like this.

I also can't wait to have my own calling cards, and to pretend I am **SPECIAL** and **IMPORTANT** and march around London visiting people. Mother and Sarah make calls all the time, Mother says they are **USEFUL** for making friends, but also for talking politics with important people. She also thinks it doesn't hurt for Sarah to be seen by some of the **BETTER FAMILIES** in our set, so that she could be introduced to single gentlemen. Though they don't want her to get married just yet. **HAHA**. Mother and Father would like Sarah to go to university to study Law or something like that. Sarah doesn't think there is much point in her getting a degree in Law when it is illegal for her to work as a lawyer. I think that is so unfair. Women are allowed to go to lots of universities, but even if they work very hard and get the **BEST MARKS** they cannot get a degree.

I would like to go to university one day. I don't suppose it matters too much if I am not allowed a degree, seeing as I want to become a detective. I'm not sure if Sherlock Holmes has one.

What about you, Christine? Would you like to go to university? I don't suppose your father would like that very much.

Yours truly,

Mary

20th May 1913

Dear Mary,

I always get a thrill when I see I have a new letter from you!

I've never thought about university. I would like to be able to continue my drawing and perhaps study some of the great painters. I know Father wouldn't like that. He thinks all artists are immoral! Jane and her mother had planned for her to go to university, but Father put a stop to that after she died. Selfishly I am glad, because now Jane teaches my lessons.

Charles and I used to take my lessons with a governess, Miss Gribble, but she wasn't anywhere near as clever as Jane. I'm not sure Father agrees with some of the things Jane is teaching me. She likes to teach me lots of interesting things about history and geography and mathematics.

"Women should be taught how to keep a home happy and comfortable," Father grumbled when I showed him a drawing of South America. I had copied from Jane's atlas. "Not how to colour in maps." Luckily, Mother jumped in and told him that will all be covered, but that if I am good at geography and mathematics I can make sure my sons get a good start with their lessons.

"Humph," said Father. But in an agreeable sort of way. Charles struggles at school and Father blames this on Miss Gribble. Sometimes he tests me at my sums at the table, though he stops over the holidays because he sees it makes Charles angry when I am able to solve problems he isn't. Bad luck, Charles!

I think you once said Sarah goes to school. Will you go? Will you board like your brother and Charles do?

Not long until the Derby now! Are you getting excited?

Yours,
Christine

Dear Christine,

I love getting your letters too! It's **WONDERFUL** to have someone who understands me. Sarah is all right as sisters go, but she thinks she is so grown up now, swooping around in her long skirt and corset. She treats me like a child!

Sarah did go to a school, but she didn't like it. Mother and Father took her out because they didn't think she was learning much. It was nothing like Edward's school. We went up to visit him for speech day last term. It looks more like a cathedral than a school and they learn all sorts of things there. I would love to go to a school like that. All the sports and getting to sleep in a room with your friends. Sarah's school sounded more like a family home. They didn't do any sports but learned lots of tosh about where a duchess should be seated at dinner and what to say if an archbishop sneezes on your salad. Do you bless them? Do you wait for them to bless you? **HAHA**. Not really, but you know the kind of thing.

Now Sarah and I study with Miss Inchpole, who teaches us all manner of things I don't think I will ever need. Sarah takes extra lessons with Father and Mother in the evening. Father is a director at a bank so is a wizard at maths and Mother was born in India so she knows a lot about geography and trade. I suppose I will take lessons with them one day. Right now I like the time to work on my drawings and to write to you, of course!

I am excited about the Derby. Especially now I have seen my dress. It isn't too awful at all, even if it isn't as grown up as I would like. We travel down on Tuesday for the race on Wednesday. I can hardly wait!

Yours truly,
Mary

P.S. I have THE MOST BRILLIANT horse joke for you!

Q: What did the jockey say to his horse after they had won the race?
A: Why the long face? HAHAHA. Because horses have long faces! Do you get it? And to have a long face means to be sad ... but they won so the horse shouldn't be sad. I'm explaining it too much. I promise, if I told you in person you would laugh yourself HORSE (hoarse)! Get it? All right, I'll stop.

5th June 1913

Dear Mary,

I have just seen the newspaper and had to write straightaway. Such horrible news from the Derby. Jane was in floods of tears. She knew Emily Davison through the WSPU.

I can't imagine what you must be feeling. Did you see it happen? Was it as quick as they said? I do hope she gets better. Though Jane tells me Emily has been unwell for ages after being in and out of prison so often.

Do write when you can!

Yours,
Christine

Look - they called her a 'suffragist'...

5th June 1913

SENSATIONAL DERBY

SUFFRAGIST'S MAD ACT

KING'S HORSE BROUGHT DOWN

WOMAN AND JOCKEY INJURED

An extraordinary incident marked the race for the Derby yesterday afternoon. As the horses were making for Tattenham Corner a woman rushed out on the course in front of the King's horse, Anmer, and put her hands above her head. The horse knocked her down, and then turned a complete somersault ... Herbert Jones. When the animal re-

Dear Christine,

Thank you for your letter. It gave me great comfort to hear from you. It was a terrible day that had started off so wonderfully.

I was wearing my lovely new dress and hat, which I had trimmed with a green and purple ribbon. I felt quite grown up, even though the skirt was not as long as I would have liked. We took a bus to Epsom Downs. Everyone on the bus was happy, hopeful that their horses would win or that they may catch a glimpse of the king himself.

Mother and Aunt Clara were wondering what the queen's hat would be like. "I think as much money could be won or lost on betting on the queen's hat as on all the horses put together," joked Father.

Taking bets on Queenie's hat! Three to one on big, white and flowery!

It was like one of the suffrage rallies. People of all classes standing side by side, chattering about how well the horses had done in previous races. We were heading towards the course when Sarah touched my shoulder.

"That's my friend Emily from the WSPU," she said, pointing towards a woman with red hair. She gave her a wave to catch Emily's attention, but Emily didn't see us. I was about to whistle to make us more obvious but Sarah **SHHHED** me. She pointed to the police. I hadn't noticed them before, but when she pointed them out I realized how many there were. "They're obviously expecting trouble," Sarah said. "Best not to draw attention to Emily. The police aren't her biggest fans."

I didn't think anything more about her until I spied her again standing near the rails at one of the bends. She had a silk scarf in her hand. White with purple-and-green stripes and the words "Votes for Women" in bold purple and green letters. I have been begging Mother to let me buy one just like that with my birthday money.

What happened next was a total blur. The horses were thundering down the course at such a speed. My brother was shouting for a horse called Craganour, as Father had put half a shilling on him to win. Mother was most annoyed as Craganour is owned by a man from a dishonourable family.[28] Mother had half a shilling on the king's horse, Anmer, who my

---

28 Craganour's owner's older brother was said to have disguised himself as a woman to take a seat in one of the lifeboats on the *Titanic*.

brother said had no chance of winning. But because of that we were watching him as he came around the bend.

"Hooray for Anmer!" cried Mother, waving her racing programme in the air.

Then Anmer was down. Someone had run out in front of him and been hit.

Half the crowd carried on cheering. They hadn't seen what had happened. Officials ran on to the course to help the jockey who had been thrown and to check on the person hit by the horse. I spotted a silk scarf lying in the grass a little way from where the person had fallen. Tugging on Sarah's sleeve, I pointed to the 'Votes for Women' scarf, my heart beating fast.

"Emily," Sarah whispered, her hand flying to her mouth.

I don't know what she could have been thinking of. Perhaps she was trying to stop the king's horse to get everyone's attention. Sarah is hopeful she'll be all right. One of the best surgeons in the country has been sent to her at Epsom Cottage Hospital. I said prayers for her at church this morning. I do hope she will be well again.

Yours truly,
Mary

Dear Mary,

We have just heard the news that Emily Davison died yesterday. It is SO sad. What a terrible thing to happen!

Father has been saying dreadful things about Emily. That she was mad and should have been locked up. He says that women are always so dramatic and emotional. When Mother spoke up at dinner last night, I nearly fell off my chair.

"Why, when women fight for what they believe in is it considered a weakness, but when men do the same it is seen as a strength?" she said.

"It is quite different!" said Father, looking very taken aback that he should have been questioned. "Quite different indeed!"

Mother has been taking extra care of Jane and is trying to keep her busy with all kinds of tasks. Jane has been very quiet, but that may be because of Father. I think if she said anything at all she might explode.

Yours,
Christine

16th June 1913

Dear Christine,

It is so awful. Sarah is **HEARTBROKEN** and Mother and Father don't know what to do with her. What hateful things for your Father to say! Jane must have been so upset. No matter how he feels about the vote, his niece's friend is dead.

Surely you must see now why women **MUST** have the vote? He is not speaking (or voting) in your mother's, Jane's or your best interests. He thinks only of himself. Women are starving themselves and putting themselves in harm's way to be heard and he just calls them all crazy. No! You must see that **CANNOT BE RIGHT**.

Sarah and Mother went to Emily's funeral a couple of days ago. I asked Sarah what it was like when she got home. She said it was beautiful. "All the white dresses and lovely flowers. Hundreds lined the street. It was like a funeral for a royal princess, not a suffragette," she told me.

Father said that Emily Davison may well have done more for the women of this country by dying than the king has done in his entire lifetime.

"It was quite wonderful. Perhaps you suffragettes aren't the wild rabble I thought you were," said Mother, wrapping her arms round me and Sarah.

Sarah and Mother have been very close since the Derby. Mother is working hard preparing for the NUWSS pilgrimage in July and Sarah has been helping her with it. I think what happened to Emily has scared her. I know it scared me. I suppose you might not have heard about the pilgrimage — it's not the sort of thing your father would read out from the paper! It's a kind of march, but much bigger and so much more **EXCITING**. Women from all over the country are marching from their homes with their local suffrage groups. There will be events in towns and cities along the way and the marchers aim to get together in Hyde Park on 26th July. Mother says **MANY THOUSANDS** of women are setting out, from as far away as Land's End in Cornwall and Newcastle.

It feels as if the nation is marching to Parliament to tell the government that this movement is bigger than a few stubborn politicians and WILL NOT BE STOPPED. Hurrah! Mother is working all day, every day getting ready for it. Sending out handbills and organizing women to make banners and sashes.

Sarah and I are helping as much as we can. We are both sewing signs and banners for the marchers! Can you believe it? **ME, SEWING!** My fingers are covered in bandages. I have literally given my blood to the cause. Haha! We're not sewing anything too fancy, like your needlework, but my sister is cutting letters and I am sewing them on. Mother has been travelling all over, taking our banners with her and making sure speakers are able to get to where they need to be. I've not seen Mother this happy for a long time.

"It's time for everyone to see that it isn't just a bunch of MAD WOMEN that support this movement," she said to me as we were folding leaflets. "But ordinary law-abiding people who want a government that represents EVERYONE. It's a march for women and men who want to make this country greater, not tear it to pieces."

I am very excited. Mother says Sarah and I can travel with her to see some of the speakers' events on the train and JOIN THE MARCHERS!

Yours truly,
Mary

22nd June 1913

Dear Christine,

How are you? I hope you aren't ill. I haven't heard from you in a while. I have to tell you what has happened since my last letter. I know I told you Mother said we could join the pilgrimage. Well, we did, we joined the women at East Grinstead. I was so excited to walk alongside them. Everyone looked so lovely in their red, white and green sashes.[29] I was very proud of mine, as I had made it myself. Spirits were high and it felt wonderful to be a part of it, but when we got further into town **EVERYTHING CHANGED**.

Mother had told me that women had been treated badly at some of the stops, but I was not prepared for what happened. Oh, Christine, it was **HORRID**! When we joined the marchers on the high street, a great crowd of men, hundreds of them, started yelling at us and throwing **TOMATOES** and **ROTTEN EGGS**! YUCK! The smell was DISGUSTING!

We broke away and took shelter in someone's house, but we couldn't stay long because some of the men broke in!

29 The colours of the NUWSS.

I was so frightened. We ran as fast as we could to a hotel, The Dorset I think it was called, and hid there until the police came.

I was so relieved to get home. The looks on the men's faces made me feel sorry for their poor mothers and sisters. It wasn't about them not wanting women to vote, they didn't want women to **SPEAK AT ALL**. Beasts!

Will you be coming to Hyde Park on the 26th? It would be so wonderful to see you again. I feel it is more important now than ever. Please say you will try to be there, it has been too long since we met in person. I have grown at least an inch since then, perhaps you won't even recognize me!

I hope I can get the stinky rotten egg smell out of my sash! Pee-eww!

Yours truly,
Mary

24th June 1913

Dear Mary,

Sorry – I wasn't ill. We just didn't have any stamps! Father kept saying he'd go out and get some, but he didn't for **aaages**. I can't help wondering if he was trying to stop me from writing to you...

Oh, Mary! I PLEADED with Mother about going to Hyde Park. I told her I wanted to be a part of history.

"But why would you want to spend time with those shouty, screechy, unnatural women?" she asked, baffled. I told her that they weren't shouty or screechy and that they are BRAVE and that it was **NATURAL** for them to want to HAVE THEIR SAY.

She knows I'm not a suffragette or likely do anything silly and she knows Jane would never let anything bad happen to me. "Although I am not sure whether I will ever want the vote, I don't want to stand in your way, Christine," she said. "Yes, you can go. Just, perhaps, don't tell your father."

Can you believe it? SHE SAID YES! I'm sure it is because Father is away for the weekend. Charles said he would tell

Father all about it as soon as he gets home, but I don't care. It will be too late by then.

Jane seems annoyed that I will be going with her though, like I have messed up her plans. She did say she would talk to Sarah and see if we can meet up afterwards for tea. It will be so wonderful to see you again! It feels like it has been for ever.

Yours truly,
Christine

P.S. Jane just came home and told me she has spoken to Sarah. We will see you in Alan's Tea Rooms, [30] at three o'clock on the 26th. I'm so excited!

30 Alan's Tea Rooms at 263 Oxford Street was a popular meeting place for suffragists and suffragettes.

27th June 1913

Dear Mary,

It was so wonderful to see you. Wasn't it just the most spectacular event? So many women, marching together! The banners were beautiful. You were right to be proud of your sash, it was lovely and it didn't smell even a little bit eggy! I wish I'd had time to make one for myself.

I was impressed by the speakers too. I have decided, I am not a suffragette, but I am a LAW-ABIDING SUFFRAGIST. I got that off one of the banners and I think it suits me. I don't agree with smashing windows, but I do believe that all men and women in this country deserve to vote.

Jane said the march was well-organized, but that she doubted it would lead to any real change. I think she enjoyed the day though. I know she always enjoys spending time with Sarah.

Please thank your mother for buying us all tea. I had not been to Alan's before, but I know Jane often meets her friends there. Perhaps we could meet there again after shopping one day?

Very best wishes,
Christine Sedgwick, Law-abiding Suffragist

30th June 1913

Dear Christine,

It was so lovely to see you, too. Wasn't the pilgrimage spectacular? Did you see in the papers that the Prime Minister has agreed with some of the organizers to discuss women getting the vote? **IMAGINE**! We might have been part of the event that leads to real change.

Father said that with so many people involved, the government would be OUT OF THEIR MINDS not to take notice, but he said that I shouldn't expect change to happen quickly. The Prime Minister wants to stay in power, and with the election coming next year, he would be unlikely to do anything that would put that at risk.

I am still hopeful though, no matter what Father says. The feeling in Hyde Park on Saturday was that change is coming. I can't believe that isn't true. Can you?

Very best wishes,
Mary

P.S. We would love to meet you at Alan's again. We could meet you on Saturday 12th, if you're not busy?

4th July 1913

Dear Mary,

We can meet you then. I have spoken with Jane and she said she would take me to Selfridges. I **ADORE** Selfridges don't you? It's so much fun to be able to wander round and touch things and try them on even if there is no way you would ever buy them.[31]

It will be nice to go out for the day. With Charles being home for the summer, the house feels quite crowded. He is becoming even more **ANNOYING**. Yesterday, when I came in from a walk with Jane, he ran straight to the piano in the drawing room and started banging on the keys.

---

31 Selfridges first opened in 1909 and was one of the first stores in England that had the stock laid out for customers to see and touch. Previously, shops kept stock behind a counter.

Put me upon an island where the girls are few.

Put me among the most ferocious lions in the zoo.

Put me in prison and I'll never fret.

But for pity's sake don't put me near a suffering-gette.

He made such a racket that Father stormed out of his study. I was hoping Charles was about to get his ears boxed,[32] but just before Father reached him, Charles began playing the song again. Father hooted and slapped the piano, saying how true it was. ARGH!

Jane walked right upstairs.

32 A slap to the side of the head. A common punishment at the time for boys and girls that behaved badly.

When I think of how wonderful the pilgrimage was and what so many women have sacrificed... How can Charles and Father make a horrid joke out of it?

I asked Jane why she didn't say something and she laughed. She **ACTUALLY LAUGHED** and said that saying something wouldn't make any difference. She said if she wanted change she would have to actually DO something. The look in her eye frightened me.

So looking forward to seeing you next Saturday!

Very best wishes,
Christine

Dear Mary,

Thank goodness you were there yesterday. I'm sorry I couldn't explain anything to you then. It was all I could do to make it to Alan's, I was in shock!

I knew Jane was up to something. She was so quiet over breakfast. Father was reading his paper, tutting at something or other.

Jane stood up, as if she was going to give a speech, "Thank you for letting me stay with you," she said. "I am grateful for all you have done."

It seemed so odd at the time, but makes perfect sense now. I thought it was even more odd when she tried to persuade me not to come into town with her.

"Are you sure you want to come?" she asked me when we were ready to leave. "The Underground will be ever so hot and stuffy. Why don't you stay in and draw?" I had to remind her that we were meeting you and Sarah at the tearooms!

"Oh, yes," said Jane. "Come along then."

We got the Tube to Marble Arch and walked up to Selfridges. The street was busy with motorcars, horses and buses. I stayed close to Jane as I didn't want to get lost in the crowd. When we reached the shop, we wandered around looking in all the different departments.

I asked Jane what she wanted to buy but she didn't seem interested in anything in particular. She just kept asking me the time. I kept pointing out the lovely gowns, but she barely seemed to notice. At half past ten, she said we should leave.

"Why?" I asked, surprised. "We're not due to meet them for another hour! I know I'm a slow walker, but I'm not that slow!" She just told me to stop asking such annoying questions.

When we were out on the street, we headed towards Alan's. A few doors down, I saw the glint of something shiny poking out of her sleeve. I couldn't make out what it was, but then she pulled the object out. It was a tiny **HAMMER**! The kind that cook uses when she makes toffee. I couldn't think why she would have it with her on Oxford Street.

She walked up to the window of a tobacco shop and **SMASHED THE WINDOW PANE.**

"Votes for women! Deeds not words!" she shouted.

I was horrified. I tried to pull her into the crowd, but she wouldn't budge. "Run and meet Mary and Sarah," she hissed. "They'll see you home. I will not set foot in your father's house again until women are given the vote."

Then she pushed me into the crowd and **SMASHED ANOTHER WINDOW.**

I didn't know what to do. The police arrived a moment later. The way they grabbed her made me cry out. She gave me a fierce look and nodded in the direction of Alan's. I wanted to stay put until another officer took my arm and yelled to Jane.

"Is this one with you?" he asked. But Jane said she'd never seen me before in her life and the officer let go of my arm.

They pulled her away towards their van. I ran to Alan's as fast as I could. I am sure I can't have made any sense when I told you what happened. I am not sure I knew myself. It was all so quick. I am so grateful for you seeing me home. I have never been on the London Underground alone. I would have got quite lost.

I am sorry Father spoke to you the way he did. He wanted you gone so he could ask about Jane. The police had already been and he didn't want the neighbours to gossip any more than they already had.

After you left I told him everything. He rushed to the police station to pay Jane's bail so that she could come home. Jane wouldn't let him. Can you believe that? She is determined to go to prison. Father was furious.

"Well, she has made her choice," Father told Mother when he got home. "I have washed my hands of that girl. She is no longer welcome in our home."

So I suppose she has her wish. I don't know what will happen to her now. If only I had known what she was planning, I could have stopped her. I hope you and Sarah got home all right.

Yours gratefully,
Christine

P.S. Do let me know if Sarah hears anything through the WSPU. Father says he will not contact the station again about Jane.

P.P.S. Sorry for writing such a long letter. I thought you both deserved a full explanation

16th July 1913

Dear Christine,

What a **HORRIBLE** thing to go through. No wonder you were so upset! I knew **SOMETHING DREADFUL** must have happened, but that is awful. I am so glad we were there!

Dearest Jane. What could she be thinking? Or rather, I suppose we know exactly what she was thinking. She wants to **FIGHT FOR THE WSPU** and go to prison with the others.

You would never have been able to talk her out of it. She is a determined woman who feels she has nothing to lose. It is because of women like her that the suffragettes will NEVER be stopped and women will NEVER be silenced.

I'm not surprised Jane refused bail. Sarah says all the suffragettes do. Going to prison is part of their service to the cause. If she had come home with your father, he would have made life dreadful for her. I think we both know Jane well enough to know that prison would seem a delightful adventure compared to that.

Yours truly,
Mary

20th July 1913

Dear Mary,

Thanks for your letter. It really helps to have such a good friend at a time like this. I feel so alone without Jane.

She has been sentenced to six months. Mother and Father wouldn't let me go to the trial. She will go to prison. I am sure she means to go on hunger strike as the others have. I know I should be proud, as this was a brave choice, but I am just so angry with her.

I miss her. Mother is unhappy. Father is angrier than ever because Mother is upset and Charles is as horrible as always.

He keeps saying awful things like, "This house is better since 'that suffering-gette' was hauled off!"

Maybe that is why Jane did it. To get away from awful Charles. Dinner this evening was so tense that I had half a mind to run into the street and set fire to something, just to get away. Sorry to be so gloomy, but I miss Jane terribly and am so worried about her. Do let me know if Sarah hears anything.

Do write soon,
Christine

25th July 1913

Dear Christine,

You poor thing. You have every right to be gloomy. I am so sorry to hear about Jane. The only comfort is that this is what she wanted. She knew what would happen. Sarah says she knows of some other members of the WSPU that were sentenced at the same time and that they will go on hunger strike, so I am sure Jane will too. I bet she wishes she had a nice big slice of cake with us at Alan's before she started smashing windows. Too soon? Probably too soon.

If she does, Mother and Father said she can stay here. We don't live far from where a lot of other women are released to recover their strength.[33] I promise we will look after her. Let your mother know. I am sure this will be a weight off her mind. Have your mother and father decided what they are going to do about your studies? With Jane gone, you won't have a governess. I **WISH** you could come and study with me and Sarah. I am sure you would make Miss Inchpole's lessons **MUCH** more entertaining.

Yours truly,

Mary

33 A house in Campden Hill, Kensington, was turned into a hospital where a lot of suffragettes could recover after they were released through the Cat and Mouse Act.

Dear Mary,

Oh, my goodness, Mary! Your letter made me feel so much better. I told Mother and she cried. She does not know how she can repay you. She loves Jane so dearly, but knows Father won't let her back in our house.

With Jane gone, I have been spending a lot of time with Mother. We are working on some handkerchiefs together. We have not spoken about it exactly, but I know they are for Jane. I have chosen the colours, purple, white and green. Jane's favourites. I think they will be quite beautiful. Not much use to her now, but I want her to see that we were thinking of her when she is free.

Father and Mother have been talking about what to do about my education.

"We could employ a new governess," suggested Mother.

"Humph," said Father. "We should send her to a small school in the countryside." Needless to say, nobody asked for MY opinion. "Jane has been a bad influence on you,"

Father said. "You need to learn what it means to be a respectable lady rather than run around London with a bunch of radicals."

I don't think they have decided anything for certain yet. I wish we could just go to school together. One like Charles' or Edward's, not Sarah's. We could have **MIDNIGHT FEASTS** (NOT midnight SNACKS) and play sport on the playing fields. Don't you think that would be fun? I think Father would prefer something more along the lines of me learning to keep my elbows off the table and walking around with a book on my head, though.[34] Boring! At least I wouldn't have to wear a **NASTY, SCRATCHY** uniform like Charles has to I suppose.

We have also been getting Charles' uniform ready for school. Sewing his name in this and that. I don't mind, as I am looking forward to him going. I like to initial Charles' school things in *swirly girly* script. Last term I dotted the 'i' of 'Sedgwick' with a little flower. He said the boys mocked him dreadfully. I was scared father would be angry, but he said it would toughen Charles up and build character.[35]

---

34 Walking with a book on your head was thought to help girls to stand up straight and walk, or rather glide, gracefully.

35 Lots of horrible things, like bullying or beatings, were considered character-building back then. Now we know that being treated unkindly just makes it more likely a person will treat others unkindly.

Any news from Jane? We are so worried about her. Do promise you will write as soon as you hear anything!

Yours,
Christine

18 August 1913

Dear Christine,

HAHA! I bet Charles looks quite the fop[36] in his uniform. We have been getting Edward's trunk ready to go back to school, too. I don't see why he can't do it himself. When women get the vote, I will vote that boys do all of their own sewing. See what I did there? Ha! There's a cause I'd go to prison for! Sewing for boys!

We got word that Jane will be released and brought to us tomorrow. I was **SO EXCITED** when I heard and have helped the maid to get her room ready. I put a pot plant on her nightstand, alongside a Sherlock Holmes novel. I do hope she hasn't already read it!

Will write soon,
Mary

36 A fop was someone who followed the latest fashion to the point of looking ridiculous.

Dear Christine,

Jane is here. Oh, Christine, she is in a **TERRIBLE** state. She is so **THIN** and **FRAIL**! I did not know what to expect, but I did not think she would be so bad.

She was brought in on a stretcher from the ambulance and put in the bed upstairs. She can barely speak! Mother has cook making all kinds of thin soups, but Jane is too weak to eat them.

There is a police officer at our door to make sure she doesn't escape. **HA**! There is **NO CHANCE** of that. Jane cannot even lift a spoon, never mind run away! I scowl at him every time I need to pass him. Sometimes I walk past just to scowl at him.

I wish I could write to you with better news. **POOR JANE**!

Yours truly,
Mary

Dear Mary,

I am **SO SAD** to hear Jane is in such an awful state. I do hope she feels stronger soon. I wish there was more I could do to help my poor cousin.

Mother was really upset when I showed her your letter. She will visit very soon but said Father has forbidden me from going with her. Please tell Jane. She knows what Father is like, so I know she will understand. I will send the handkerchief I have made with Mother and perhaps some sweet treats.

Jane has a sweet tooth. Perhaps you could tell your cook that?

Yours truly,
Christine

26th August 1913

Dear Christine,

I told cook about Jane's sweet tooth and she made a batch of her **DELICIOUS** madeleine cakes. Jane really **PERKED UP** when she took a couple in to her. She is still weak but is managing to eat a little more every day.

Your mother came yesterday while I was out with Sarah. Mother said she was very upset when she left. But you will not believe what arrived for Jane today! A certificate signed by **EMMELINE PANKHURST** herself. It is **BEAUTIFULLY DECORATED** with green leaves and purple and white flowers. It thanks her for her service to the women's movement. Sarah told me that it was designed by Sylvia Pankhurst.[37]

I took it up to Jane as soon as it arrived. I think she was pleased, as she lifted her head off the pillow to look at it. I am glad she is a bit better, but I dread to think of her being taken back to prison. The police ask after her every day and I almost don't want her to get well as we will no longer be able to keep her safe.

Yours truly,
Mary

37 The daughter of Emmeline Pankhurst, and a talented artist.

6th September 1913

Dear Mary,

I am so glad you are there to care for Jane. How exciting for her to get a certificate! I am scared of Jane going back to prison, too. There must be something we can do to stop that happening. Mother has an aunt near Edinburgh who asked after Jane in a letter last week. It turns out this aunt is rather a fan of the suffragettes! I had a crazy idea that if we could sneak Jane past the police officer we could put her on a train up to Edinburgh. I don't know how we would manage it, but I would love to be able to do something.

What do you think?

Yours truly,
Christine

P.S. Charles may be going back to school soon, but he won't be escaping the suffragettes. We just received word that his school was damaged by two fires! WSPU leaflets were posted around the local area, so it must have been the suffragettes.

Dear Christine,

I hope your mother managed to pass this note to you without your father seeing! My goodness, your letter got me thinking.

Do you think you might be able to convince your mother to bring you to Alan's on Saturday at one o'clock? We can talk more then. I have a plan and I'm calling it 'OPERATION AFTERNOON TEA'.

Yours truly,
Mary

P.S. Jane is looking much better, which is why I think we should meet as soon as possible.

P.P.S. I do hope the school fire doesn't stop Charles from going back. Your family have sacrificed enough for voting rights. You shouldn't have to put up with more of Charles to boot. And if you do, you should certainly get more than a medal!

10th September 1913

Dear Mary,

Hopefully my Mother has given this letter to your maid when she popped round! Just a quick note to say I have spoken to Mother and she has agreed to bring me to Alan's. I told her it was the least we could do after all your family were doing for Jane.

I can't wait to hear about **OPERATION AFTERNOON TEA**.

See you on Saturday,
Christine

13th September 1913

Dear Mary,

It was **WONDERFUL** to see you and Sarah on Saturday. I can hardly believe it, but Mother has thought about it and agreed with **OPERATION AFTERNOON TEA**. She said she has to do something for Jane, so she will help in any way she can. She has written to Aunt Portia in Edinburgh and is sure she will send someone to meet Jane's train.

She asked me to write and tell you that she would like to visit Jane again on the 24th at midday. Thank you again, Mary. Mother said she thought you would make an excellent detective with all your scheming.

Yours truly,
Christine

Dear Christine,

Operation Afternoon Tea was a **COMPLETE SUCCESS**! Jane is gone! Your mother played her part wonderfully, you would have been so proud of her. I will tell you everything that happened and leave nothing out. Then **BURN** this letter like you did for the **CASE OF THE MIDNIGHT SNACK**! I'm not sure it's quite normal for eleven-year-old girls to be part of such secret and important operations and setting fire to their letters all the time! It's all very exciting.

Your mother arrived at midday as you said she would. I ran to the window as I didn't want to miss a thing. She walked up to our steps, nodding to the policeman watching the house (I swear he is always there. Does he never need to use the water closet?). Mother showed her to Jane's room.

Mother said I mustn't go in, so I listened from the top of the stairs instead. There was much toing and froing and Jane struggled to get into a dress your mother had brought. Your mother put Jane's nightgown on.

"I'm rather looking forward to an afternoon in bed," your mother joked.

Jane and my mother laughed. I don't think I have ever heard Jane laugh. Then again, I don't suppose she has had much to laugh about for a while.

When Jane came out wearing your mother's dress, I did a double take. Her time in prison has made her face look older and not eating has made her look quite gaunt. She gave me a wink and then pursed her lips in the way you told me your mother does. I swear her usually pink mouth lost all of its colour. Jane and your mother really do look so much alike. I felt certain the police officer would think Jane was your mother. He would have had to look very closely to see what we had done! **HAHA**!

Oh, Jane was so bold. Though she had a lace handkerchief to her face, I swear she looked right at the officer and gave him the slightest nod. I held my breath. What if he realized who she was? That it was Jane and not your mother! What if he was to notice your suffragette stitching on her handkerchief? Yes, Christine! That was the handkerchief she chose! To think careful stitches could have undone the whole operation! Haha!

But he didn't recognize her. She stepped up into the waiting car and drove off down the street. When she turned the corner, I finally breathed again. What a day!

Once we were sure Jane had made it to her train to Scotland, your mother got dressed in the spare clothes she had brought with her. The police officer hadn't suspected anything or come to check 'Jane' was still in bed, so there was no need for her to stay.

She took each of our hands in hers, and said she was **SO GRATEFUL** for everything we had done for Jane. As soon as she stepped outside, the police officer looked very confused. Had he not seen Mrs Sedgwick leave hours ago? He took hold of your mother's arm and asked her to come back into the house with him.

"I'm in rather a hurry, officer!" said your mother.

But the officer was having none of it. "If you'll just step back inside for a moment, madam."

He pulled her back into the house and ran up the stairs to Jane's room.

When he found the bed empty, he thundered back down the stairs and dashed out to raise the alarm. There were officers everywhere, running about like headless chickens. It felt wonderful, though I was a little bit scared our mothers would get into trouble. They were **MARVELLOUS** though. You'd have thought butter wouldn't melt!

"Jane must have sneaked out while we were busy gossiping in the parlour," your mother told him. "You know what we ladies are like when we start, officer!"

The officers seemed more interested in where Jane was to pay too much attention to their story. But Jane was already well on her way to Scotland. Haha!

Anyway, I'm sure your mother filled you in on the rest. **WHAT A DAY!** I had to write to you to let you know. Today was a real victory for women. **DEEDS NOT WORDS**!

Yours excitedly,
Mary

Dear Mary,

I am so pleased Jane is free! Mother gave me a nod when she came in, so I guessed everything went to plan. I've not had a chance to talk to her properly. I hope Jane finds some peace in Scotland, though I am sure she will be up to her old tricks in no time.

But I have bad news. The police came to our house this evening to ask Mother about her part in Jane's escape. Father looked so shocked when they were led into the drawing room.

"We haven't heard from my niece, officer," he told them. "We will of course inform you if we do."

He did not know that Jane had made her escape and he certainly did not know that Mother and I had helped her.

"Pardon me, sir," said an officer, "but we would like to question your wife about her involvement. We have reports that she helped your niece escape."

I was sent upstairs, so I couldn't hear anything.

When the officers finally left nearly two hours later,

Father was angrier than I have ever heard him! And that's saying something, as you know. "I would **NEVER** have believed that you could have brought such **DISGRACE** on the family," he shouted. "After all I **HAVE DONE**, taking in your sister and her daughter!"

He said that it was too late for Jane now, but that there was still time for me to learn to become a lady. He said I must be sent to a proper school immediately.

Charles had been listening in and barged into my room, delighted I was being sent off to school.

"All the other girls are going to think you're a dunce," he said. "Nobody will want to sit next to a 'suffering-gette'."

I told him he was a **BEAST.** "You're the dunce! You're not smart enough to have your own opinions! You just COPY FATHER'S!" Charles didn't seem to be able to think of anything to say to that. No surprise there. **HA!**

I can barely write the worst part, though, Mary. Father said I must never see or write to you **EVER AGAIN**. He said that if he found that I had disobeyed him he would send me to school very far away from Mother and not let me home, even for the holidays. Can you believe it? He said it was his duty as my father to keep me away from bad influences and to make sure I become a useful member of society.

I just wept. He said I must not write to Jane either and must tell him if I ever get word from her. My heart is breaking, Mary, to think I will have to go through all of this without my best friend to tell my secrets to. I can't believe this will be my last ever letter to you. Promise me you won't forget me, Mary. I could not bear it if I thought this was the end of everything we have been to each other.

Yours truly,
Christine

1st October 1913

Dear Christine,

My dear, **DEAR** friend. Of course I will **NEVER** forget you! How could I ever forget my best friend? I am so sorry your father has forbidden us from writing to one another! I hope he changes his mind, but from what you have told me, he is almost as stubborn as Jane. Haha.

I made you a handkerchief so that you may remember me and our friendship. Look at the **HIDDEN MESSAGE** along the hem! Without you I would never have believed I could have done such delicate stitches. I thought you could take it with you to your new school, wherever it is.

You will forever be in my heart dear friend; I know for a fact that we will meet again someday. And you **MUSTN'T** worry about Jane. She has written

to Mother and says she is feeling better every day. She is desperate to return to London. She wanted me to make sure to tell you to study hard at school and wait to hear from her, as she will find a way to contact you as soon as she can. I don't doubt that for one minute. Any plan of your father to keep you apart will be no match for Jane, or your mother for that matter. Haha!

Do try to write when and if you can, dear friend.

Mary
Your most loyal friend and suffragette

P.S. When I am a real detective, I will make it one of my cases to find you. Never fear. You have not seen the last of Detective Inspector M. Forrest.

14th August 1914

Dear Christine,

It feels so long since I last wrote. I know that I shouldn't send this letter, in case you get into trouble with your father. I even tried to disguise my handwriting on the envelope! **HAHA**. I can't tell you how much I have missed your letters. I hate not knowing what you are doing, especially now when things are so uncertain. Can you believe we are at war?[37] I'm not sure what that means, but I am so frightened of what is to come. Mother thinks it will all be over by Christmas (HURRAH!) but Father isn't so sure (BOO!).

There is some lighter news, though! Did you see the government have said they will let the suffragettes out of prison? We have not heard from Jane since the news (have you?), but this means she could come back to London and not face being locked up! Isn't that wonderful?

Sarah said Mrs Pankhurst has told everyone in the WSPU that they must do what they can to support the war effort

---

37 On 4th of August 1914, Great Britain declared war on Germany. The British government released all suffragettes not long after and pardoned those that had been released under the Cat and Mouse Act. Mrs Pankhurst ordered members of the WSPU to stop all violent activity on the 13th of August 1914 and support the war effort.

and not smash any more windows or set fire to anything. Sarah said some members didn't seem too happy about it, but that she agrees that they need to do everything they can to help us win the war.

I hope that you get this and you can write back to me. Do write if you can!

Yours truly,
Mary

EPILOGUE
1918

Dear Mary,

At last, women have the vote! Were you there? I looked everywhere for you. I felt sure you wouldn't miss such a glorious occasion. Mrs Pankhurst addressing the Albert Hall! Celebrating that women finally have the right to vote! I went with Jane – and Mother! Ha! I know! Would you believe it? Mother said after all the work women have done in the service of this country,[38] giving them the vote is the very least the government can do.

38 With so many men away fighting in Europe, the women left behind took on a lot of jobs traditionally done by men. These jobs included driving busses, working in factories, farm work and firefighting.

I'm not sure I ever believed this day would come., after all the excitement before the Great War. I worried that it had all been **FORGOTTEN**, but no. The WSPU may have stopped their war against the government, but they had not stopped their work towards justice and real change.

I sobbed all the way through the hymn, 'Oh God, Our Help in Ages Past'. I'm not sure how anyone managed to sing. Haha. The orchestra played with such passion. I know that I was not the only one in tears. Perhaps Father was right when he said women were too emotional to be given the vote. **HAHA**.

And then Mrs Pankhurst took to the stage. There she stood, the great lady, who has given so much to get the vote. The crowd went wild with cheering. I thought they would never let her speak, but then she started, pausing after each sentence to let the crowd clap and cheer (and blow their noses, loudly). I remember you wrote to me after hearing her speak at Chelsea, all those years ago. You were right. She is a marvellous speaker.

I really hope you and your family are well, Mary. It would be wonderful to meet. Alan's isn't there anymore, did you know?

Do write back when you can!

Yours truly,
Christine

Dearest Christine,

I cannot tell you how happy I was to receive your letter! **ALMOST** as happy as when I heard women would finally have the vote! Haha!

I would LOVE to meet. I have thought about you SO MUCH over the years. The war has taken so much from so many that I am so pleased that it hasn't taken you from me. But, Christine, you sound just the same in your letter. I hope this means we can start writing to one another again! I shall try my **ABSOLUTE HARDEST** not to be a terrible influence! Haha!

How about we meet outside Selfridges on Saturday at eleven o'clock? Why don't we call it **OPERATION SHOPPING TRIP** for old time's sake? Do let me know if you can come. I want to know everything, and I have so much to tell you! **HAHA!**

Yours always,
Mary

P.S. I was there, with Mother and Sarah. It was wonderful. I'm not surprised I didn't see you though, I could barely see the stage through my tears and I couldn't sing any of the hymns for sobbing. What a glorious time to be alive! Women have the vote and my best friend is mine once more!

HISTORICAL
NOTE

True or False?

False

Mary, Christine and their families didn't really exist, though families a lot like theirs certainly did. In reality, it would have been difficult for the postman to deliver Mary and Christine's letters at the speed they wrote them in this story – but events were unfolding so quickly in 1913 that it's easy to imagine letters just like these flying back and forth London. Whoosh!

True

In 1913, women were not allowed to vote in elections and a lot of people (men and women) were very angry about that. Emmeline Pankhurst was a real person – she led a group called the WSPU, whose members were nicknamed 'suffragettes'. She really did call them to commit acts of vandalism in her name, including digging up golf courses and setting fire to summer houses. Many of the women were arrested, and lots of them went on hunger strike to protest and were force-fed in the way described in the story. Sadly, Emily Davison really did die as a result of her injuries at the Epsom Derby.

Take a look at the timeline on the next pages to see some of the real events that inspired Mary and Christine's story, and discover where we are with women's rights today.

Operation Change the World!

Although much has changed since Mary and Christine's time there is still much to do. Women in the UK still earn on average 10% less than men in similar jobs. That's the same as a woman having to work over a month more each year than a man to get the same pay! Yikes! Also, fewer than a third of the top jobs in the country are held by women, despite the fact that more girls than boys go to university each year.

In some places across the world, there are rules as to what women are allowed to wear, what medical treatment they are allowed to receive and where they are allowed to go. In lots of countries, girls are unable to get as good an education as boys; instead they are expected to look after their homes and younger siblings.

What Mary, Christine, Jane and Sarah's story tells us, is that when girls work together anything can happen.

Timeline to Change

1870: The first bill concerning votes for women failed in Parliament.

1897: The National Union of Women's Suffrage Society (NUWSS) was formed, under the leadership of Millicent Fawcett.

1903: Emmeline Pankhurst formed the Women's Social and Political Union (WSPU).

1905: First suffragettes arrested for disturbing a Liberal Party meeting. WSPU militancy began.

1909: Marion Dunlop was the first suffragette to go on hunger strike in prison. She spent 91 hours refusing food, and was then released due to ill health. Shortly after, the force-feeding of prisoners was introduced.

1911: Emily Wilding Davison was the first suffragette to set fire to a postbox. Many other members of the WSPU followed suit.

1912: The WSPU began to use fire as a weapon, burning down railway stations, cricket pavilions, racecourse stands and golf clubhouses in an 'arson campaign'.

1913: In February, the suffragettes set fire to the country house of the Chancellor of the Exchequer, David Lloyd George. In April, the Temporary ischarge for Ill Health Act (the Cat and Mouse Act) was introduced. Rather than force-feeding suffragettes on hunger strike, the women were now released when the strike began to affect their health. They were then given some time to recover, before being arrested again and taken back to prison. In June, Emily Wilding Davison stepped out in front of the king's horse at the Epsom Derby and died four days later in hospital. Later that June, the NUWSS Pilgrimage began, with women all over the UK marching for the right to vote The march ended in Hyde Park on 26th July.

1914: Britain declared war on Germany and the First World War began. The government released suffragette prisoners and Emmeline Pankhurst told the WSPU to stop militant action and instead work towards the war effort.

1918: The Representation of the People Act was introduced. This gave the right to vote to women aged 30 and over who were householders, wives of householders, owned property worth more than £5 (that's about £460 in today's money) or who had graduated from a university.

1919: Nancy Astor became first female Member of Parliament.

1928: The Equal Franchise Act was introduced. It gave the right to vote to all women aged 21 and over.

1929: Margaret Grace Bondfield became first female cabinet minister.

1969: The second Representation of the People Act lowered the voting age from 21 to 18. This is the still the legal voting age in the UK today.

1979: Margaret Thatcher became the first female Prime Minister in the UK.

Heroines from History

Emmeline Pankhurst

1858-1928

Emmeline Pankhurst founded the Women's Social and Political Union (WSPU) in 1903 and campaigned for women's suffrage alongside her daughters Sylvia and Christabel Pankhurst. Emmeline Pankhurst went to prison many times for her actions and encouraged members of the WSPU to do the same. Emmeline Pankhurst was an excellent public speaker and travelled all over the world giving speeches on women's rights. She died in 1928, shortly before women in the United Kingdom were granted full voting rights.

Millicent Garrett Fawcett

1847-1929

Millicent Fawcett was the leader of National Union of Women's Suffrage Societies (NUWSS) from 1897–1919. She believed women's right to vote could be achieved by working with politicians, rather than by smashing windows, though she was said to admire the courage of the suffragettes. Millicent Fawcett devoted more than 60 years of her life to the cause and was in the House of Commons in 1928 when women were finally granted full voting rights.

Emily Wilding Davison

1872-1913

Emily Davison joined the WSPU in 1906. She broke the law in the name of women's suffrage by setting fire to postboxes, throwing rocks at the Chancellor's carriage and spending the night in the House of Commons. She went to prison many times and was treated very badly, including almost being drowned in her cell and being force fed. Emily Davison died in Epsom Cottage Hospital from the injuries she received at the 1913 Derby.

After the accident, Emily Davison's scarf was picked up by a course steward. This steward is said to have attended Emily Davison's funeral carrying his baby daughter carefully wrapped in her scarf.

Lilian Lenton

1891-1972

Like Jane in the story, Lilian Lenton was arrested and taken to prison many times. She went on hunger strike and, unlike Jane, she was force-fed. After the Cat and Mouse Act, Lilian was released into the care of friends in Birmingham, only to escape recapture in a way similar to OPERATION AFTERNOON TEA! Lilian escaped so many times that she became known to the police as the 'Tiny Wily Elusive Pimpernel'.

If you enjoyed *My Best Friend the Suffragette*, why not try...

I Was There...

Step back into
Victorian England

ROYAL NURSEMAID

I Was There...

Step back onto
the most famous
ship in history

TITANIC

I Was There...

Step back into
the trenches of the
First World War

ALONE IN THE TRENCHES